Other titles in this series

Tales of the Tamworth Two
Wanted – Two Little Pigs

The Great Escape
THE TRUE STORY OF THE TAMWORTH TWO

Butch and Sundance now live happily at Badzel Park Farm, near Tonbridge in Kent,
which is owned by The Wildside Trust

First published in Great Britain by Madcap Books, André Deutsch Ltd, 76 Dean Street, London, W1V 5HA
André Deutsch is a subsidiary of VCI plc
www.vci.co.uk

Text and illustrations copyright © 1998 Madcap Books
The Tamworth Two appear by arrangement with the Daily Mail
A catalogue record for this title is available from the British Library

ISBN 0 233 99505 6

Reprographics by Jade Reprographics Ltd, Braintree.
Printed by Proost nv in Belgium

Two Little Pigs Make Friends

By Lesley Young · Gyles Brandreth
Illustrated by Julie Dene

MADCAP

Butch and Sundance were rolling in the mud.

'Do you remember our great escape?' said Sundance.
'Isn't it good to feel safe at last?'

'Yes, but I had a bad dream last night,' said Butch.
'I dreamt we were being chased again and we had to
hide under a bush in the freezing cold. I couldn't stop
shaking. I've been giving myself a good rub against
the fence. But look – I'm still shaking.'

'Relax. All we have to do now
   is enjoy ourselves,' said Sundance.
         'Look!' he squeaked. 'Here comes the hose!'
         The two little pigs raced down the field.

They chased each other round in circles
while the water gushed down on them.
It fell like a cool shower on their
backs. It trickled off the ends of their snouts.
And it washed all the mud from their
coats and made their ginger bristles
sparkle in the sun.

'So that's what you look like,' grunted Butch. 'I had forgotten there was a handsome pig under all that mud.'

But Sundance didn't answer. He was staring in horror at Butch's coat.

The water had washed away all the mud and he could see large patches where Butch's bristles had been rubbed off.

There was only one word for these patches.
And the word was BALD.

Butch poked her snout
out of the sty.

'I'm not coming out until my coat grows back,' she grunted.
'I may have to stay in here for ever.'

Sundance wandered off, but it was no fun chasing his own tail and he lay down and put his head between his trotters.
A rabbit popped up in front of him. 'You look very sad. Can I help?' the rabbit asked.

Sundance told him what the problem was.

'Is that all?' chuckled the rabbit. 'Leave it to me.'
And off he hopped.

Soon, a surprised-looking face appeared over the pigs' fence.

'I have a present for you,' he said. He disappeared and came up again with his mouth full of white wool which he threw into the pigs' field.

'I am a llama,' he said, 'and a llama has his coat trimmed in hot weather. I have brought you some of the wool.'

Sundance took it in to Butch. She opened one eye and looked at it. 'A woolly rug? That will cover one bald patch.'

The next day, a beautiful scaly creature walked along the top of the fence.

'Look who's here,' called Sundance, but Butch stayed in the sty.

'I am an iguana,' said the creature, 'and I have brought you some of my scales.'

Butch trotted out of the sty. 'Do we put these on your back?' asked Sundance.

'No! She's not an iguana,' said the iguana. 'But they could be earrings…'

Butch put them on.

A snake slithered up. 'Here's my old s-skin,' he hissed. 'Wear it as a s-scarf.'

Butch and Sundance were asleep in their sty when a loud cry woke them up.

A bright blue and green bird was perched on their fence. The two little pigs rushed out to see him. He spread his tail feathers into a huge fan. Butch was so amazed that she forgot all about her bald patches.

'I hear we're dressing you up,' said the bird to Butch, 'and you can't be really dressed without peacock feathers.' The peacock bowed and gave Butch a couple of feathers from his tail.

A sheep with floppy ears came up behind him and said, moving her mouth as if she was chewing her words, 'Now, take this wool and tell me if it is softer than the wool from that llama…'

Butch sat in the grass, covered in all her presents.

A hedgehog crept up and said in a tiny voice, 'I don't think you'd want any of my spikes, but I gathered some flowers for you.'

The flowers sat on Butch's head like a crown. Sundance stared at her. 'Your coat has grown back,' he said. 'You can take these things off now.'

'Don't be silly – I'm keeping them on for the party,' said Butch.

'Party? What party?' squeaked Sundance.

'What party?' laughed Butch, as the two little pigs' new friends crowded into the field. 'Our party, of course!'